A Thanksgiving Tale

Blue Paws on Main Street

Written by Joan Thomson Kretschmer
Drawings by Joan Lewis

• Chicago •

A Thanksgiving Tale

Blue Paws on Main Street
Written by Joan Thomson Kretschmer
Drawings by Joan Lewis

Published by
Joshua Tree Publishing
• Chicago •
JoshuaTreePublishing.com

13-Digit ISBN: 978-1-956823-02-8

Cover Image Credit: ©Jenifoto

Disclaimer:
This is a work of fiction. Names, characters, places, and incidents are the product of the author's imagination or have been used fictitiously. Any resemblance to actual persons, living or dead, events, locales or organizations is entirely coincidental.

Printed in the United States of America

Dedication

In memory of my father, Samuel M. Lewis, a brilliant immigrant fleeing from murderous Cossacks. A shy person who was adventurous and daring; a survivor, self-taught, who achieved the American dream and financial success. A generous soul who opened the umbrella of his kindness to shelter family, relatives, and strangers. A unique, patriotic, grateful contributor to his adopted land, and a deeply religious man. Above all, an honest, principled individual who believed in truth.

He lived by and taught me:
"Justice, justice, shall you pursue."

Table of Contents

Foreword

This book is a modest proposal for an evolving, reinvigorated, all-encompassing celebration of Thanksgiving and our many blessings through the tale of a small town's successful battle to overcome grime, slime, and time. It is based on a true story.

Let us reconsider the gifts we take for granted, such as clean water, fresh air, freedom of the press, the rule of law, science, unity, diversity, and much more.

In this story, like Dickens's *Bleak House*, decades roll by. This case features a factory owner's poisonous pollution, stonewalling, indifference, and legal skirmishes that adversely affect the inhabitants. The bottom line is the protection of human life and the environment, achieved thanks to many forms of human ingenuity and cooperation.

The leitmotif is "Justice, justice shall ye pursue."

Chapter 1: Discoveries

Biffy was standing in her small, fragrant garden with clippers in her hand. "The last roses of summer," she said, smiling as she gathered velvety-soft, scented pink petals into her straw Nantucket basket.

"Welcome to Ludwigshaven, Leonora! New in town, I hear," she added in a cheery tone, putting down her clippers, removing her dusty floral gardening gloves, and extending the delicate, small-boned fingers of her right hand. "Stacey tells me that you had quite a terrifying experience at the Ludwig Factory yesterday."

Lithe, agile, slender, white-haired, and well into her seventies, Biffy Revere had been fondly dubbed the town philosopher, the walking repository of its history, and a welcomed-if-loquacious narrator. With charm, a cutting intellect, life-long-honed people skills, and an occasionally sharp tongue, she was a respected community leader.

"I thought Leonora and her family should meet you and find out the truth," Stacey interjected. A buxom woman in her early forties, with curly black hair, she turned to Leonora. "Biffy and her family have lived here for generations. There is no one more capable of explaining."

"I'm flattered, thanks, although it is true," Biffy chuckled as she greeted Leonora's family.

With a slight tilt of her head, she motioned to follow her up onto the large screened front porch, where they settled into white wicker rocking chairs. Refreshments for her guests were waiting on the wicker coffee table: tall crystal pitchers of icy lemonade and sun tea, a platter of fresh-baked butter cookies, cobalt-blue glasses, and white paper napkins with blue and yellow tulips.

"Let's start with a little background," Biffy said. "My ancestors came in the seventeenth century, and Paul Revere was one of my relatives. Stacey wasn't kidding when she said our family has been here for generations.

"I remember Charles Ludwig. He was born and grew up here in Ludwigshaven and loved this tiny coastal town when it had only a general store. Old New England, picturesque, but poor. His name is no coincidence. He was a descendant of the original Ludwigs, founders who emigrated from Germany in the nineteenth century. In the early twentieth century, Charles went off into the world, became a railroad magnate, and returned to share his wealth with those who had raised him. Yes, our favorite son came home, built the Ludwig Library, Ludwig Y, Ludwig Auditorium, Ludwig Hospital, Ludwig Boat Dock, Ludwig High, Ludwig Park, Ludwig Town Hall,

Ludwig Arboretum, and several other Ludwig municipal buildings.

"He died decades ago, but his memory lives on for many reasons. At six feet, eleven inches, he made a big impression, created an enormous fortune, and left an extraordinary legacy—all the results of his towering intellect and big heart. He was a man of exceptional generosity, a leader in the nation, and a friend of Mark Twain.

"But all that is just part of the story. To boost the economy, he imported a business, expanded it, and constructed the Ludwig Factory on ten acres of previously unused land. He hired almost all the local adult citizens and even thoughtfully provided them with the Ludwig Recreation Hall, right on the grounds, for relaxation and socialization between or after shifts. I worked there myself.

"His July 4th celebrations on the property for the townspeople were legendary. Everyone attended, from newborns to centenarians, and all went home with baskets of goodies and armloads of souvenirs.

"If one could top that off, Ludwig did: his Thanksgiving festivities were *the* event of the year. How proud his ancestors would have been . . . and how proud of him and of burgeoning, growing Ludwigshaven his fellow residents became in its heyday. But more about all that later.

"After Charles passed away, the buildings in his name remained, but the factory was purchased by a new owner, William Wigglesworth, a five-foot-four-inch individual described by employees and local residents as mean, nasty, brutish, short, angry, argumentative, and self-centered. A human hawk always hunting for new prey, driven by the great god Mammon and internal demons. His cold blue eyes could freeze you on the spot, and at his most relaxed, his pursed lips settled into his usual haughty smirk of derision.

"Under Wigglesworth's aegis, the Ludwig Factory hummed on for a while and then closed abruptly, with quite a scandalous story of greed, indifference, legal battles, and destruction attached to its demise *and continuing to this very day.* The majority of Ludwigshaven's citizens were suddenly unemployed, without health insurance, pensions, and insurance. After decades of earning a secure living, many residents had to cope, to look elsewhere for jobs. Today, many commute to neighboring towns or into the city for employment," Biffy said, pausing.

"A veritable melting pot of chemicals is streaming and stewing on those many acres," Stacey added. "Arsenic, asbestos, and wastes containing cyanide and heavy metals, copper and nickel, polychlorinated biphenyls (PCBs), and acids. We call it Wiggle-swamp! We have been trying to get him to clean it up."

Sad to say, dear reader, after Wigglesworth arrived in Ludwigshaven, July Fourth reverted simply to a day off for the family; and the last Thursday in November became a quiet, private holiday. As summer melted into fall, the harsh New England air may have been lit with sunlight but became bone-chilling. And the hearts of local residents—once warmed by a festive, kind, welcoming

Charles Ludwig—turned inwards. Frost coated the yellowing beach grasses. The sandy soil became hard and crusted. Ducks hid and foraged in the icy waters, and geese alighted temporarily along their migration to the south. The annual football game was played, as done in numerous towns across the continent. Some watched a parade on TV, and families met for dinners in homes with memories of former Ludwig celebrations becoming fodder for old-timers' narratives.

"You saw the factory yesterday. Please tell me what happened to you, Leonora," Biffy asked.

Chapter 2:
Leonora Explores

It was the morning after Labor Day, and Leonora was standing near purple-blue hydrangea bushes in front of a freshly painted, sprawling Victorian house. A slight chill was in the fresh salt air, a sure sign of the waning of summer and the anticipatory excitement of an unfurling fall.

"I was watching the long lines of cars heading along Main Street, threading their way toward the city," Leonora began, "and I was thinking about a new school year in a new town."

A teenager, wondering who her new teachers and friends would be. Could she play in the band for football games? Soon golden orange and red leaves would drift to the ground and, with the help of the wind, deposit piles for jumping—and nuisances for homeowners. In an instant, her stream of consciousness flowed to Halloween and instantly on to Thanksgiving, candied sweet potatoes with luscious raisins, melt-in-your-mouth pumpkin pie, warm soft cornbread, and her relatives gathering and celebrating.

"A day to give thanks," her parents' oft-repeated words were suddenly in her mind.

"It was a gorgeous day, and I was feeling happy, with lots to give thanks for: a wonderful family, a new home, my beloved cat, Peanut Butter."

She moved toward the gray wooden steps, cupped her hands to direct her voice upward, and called out: "May I go and explore now, Mom?" She knew the answer would be yes but politely followed the family's rule: "Always let others know where you are so they will not worry unnecessarily."

Laura peered out of an open upper-story window, paintbrush in hand. She and her husband, Wolfgang Wright, had recently moved to Ludwigshaven, drawn by the affordable real estate and a quiet location off the beaten path. The quaint architecture, grassy marshlands, and bay beyond were attractions and incentives. An artist and a writer, she and he could work from home, and for cultural endeavors, the city was less than an hour away. A great place to rear their children who could walk to school, ride bikes, and roam freely and independently without the chaperoning required of city parents.

"I had finished unpacking, and I couldn't wait to see what was nearby. I knew my mom was busy, so I promised to report to her and perhaps come back for her later to do more exploring later," Leonora added. "I wanted to go by myself but was trying to be inclusive. Since I was a small child, I've loved taking walks with my mother, especially when we were in a new place. But yesterday, I had no time to wait. I was bursting with curiosity."

"Run along and have fun," Laura sang out in a clear, upbeat, merry tone. "Scout out the neighborhood but don't get lost. See you later . . ."

Relieved and released, Leonora skipped along the flagstone path to the sidewalk, turned right, and headed off, like the bear who went over the mountain, to see what she could see––with the tune echoing in her inner ear. Passing neat little gardens, trimmed hedges, and dogs that barked protectively and often ominously, she studied the quiet wooden houses divided by tire-marked sandy driveways—her new neighborhood.

Tasting and testing her freedom, Leonora turned left at the second corner onto Mayflower Drive, a broad street with a grassy, sandy island in the center. Soon after, another left loomed with a green-and-white street sign for Miles Standish Road, a narrow lane with small weathered-gray Cape Cod houses. Within a block, Samoset Road intersected.

"I love history, and one after the next, on and on, were names familiar to me from my American history class!" Leonora explained to Biffy.

The local population was clearly remembering and honoring the Pilgrims and their journey on the Mayflower to the New World—or more exactly to what is now known as Plymouth and Duxbury.

"I had read Governor Bradford's account of their travels and establishment of the Plimouth Plantation,"

Leonora continued with excitement. "Could I be walking in the actual footsteps of early founders of the nation? Much to discover and learn . . . How very interesting. Thanksgiving this year would be celebrated near *where it all happened*."

Out of the corner of her eye, she detected her adored pet, Peanut Butter, padding along at a distance behind, stealthily sniffing and peering but keeping pace as she was wont to do when trailing after family members on walks. Not terribly surprised to find she had a companion of sorts, Leonora stopped, kneeled down to pat the luxurious calico fur coat, and gently passed her hand from head to tail across the orange, black, and white patterns.

Resuming, the pair of walkers reached an enormous field surrounded on the periphery by shabby wire fencing. There was a sprawling complex with old wooden and brick structures: a central large empty New England factory and smaller outbuildings with broken windows and slumping roofs. A ragged sign fluttered with blood-red and coal-black letters on a white background, silently cautioning: "Ludwig Factory: DO NOT ENTER!"

Suddenly Peanut Butter skirted through a hole in the fencing and was picking up speed. Who could blame her? After all, she was a cat, not an intentional violator. A curious creature who could not read––nor cared to read–– intent on exploring like her mistress, and true to her species, not turning back when summoned.

Close by a shaky wire closure in the rusting fence, a kind of door was hanging loosely, held in place by several strands of rope. Carefully removing the ties and stepping slowly, lest it topple onto her, Leonora slipped through the opening and ran to chase after her feline family member that was already romping without restraint across the vast muddy, pebbly property and dashing through a yellow liquid patch shimmering in the sun.

"Come here," Leonora laughed. "'You little rascal, you! We are not allowed here. This is not your playground." She scooped up Peanut Butter in her arms and turned back to retrace her steps and slip through the fence opening.

"Look at you. Your paws are covered in blue gunk, and your tummy looks as if it has been painted yellow! Enough. I am carrying you home," she added lovingly. "Much as you don't like bathing," she warned, "that's what is in the cards for you as soon as possible." She hugged the precious bundle and began to run. "Samoset to Standish to Mayflower, and we'll be there as fast as my feet will carry me."

Chapter 3: Vetting

"Where have you been?" Laura looked directly at Peanut Butter with dismay as Leonora deposited the furry bundle in the kitchen sink. "I've used many kinds of paint in my life, but I've never seen anything like this. Where did you pick up this blue slime on your paws? How did you get this yellow goo on your coat?"

As if a cat could answer. Treated, loved, and admired, the little pet was spoken to often about many subjects as if she were almost human. Peanut Butter hissed, and it took four dedicated hands to hold her down and try to wash her fur.

During that dramatic event, amidst more menacing hisses and plaintive meows, Franz Wright, Leonora's twin, bounded into the kitchen, football jersey dripping with sweat, shoulder pads in hand.

"Hi, Mom! Hey, sis, what's happening?" he asked, suddenly noticing a stranger seated at the kitchen table.

"And there was Stacey Lincoln, our new neighbor," Leonora explained.

Stacy had come over to welcome the Wrights before the energetic entry of the younger generation and had been enjoying fresh mint tea and sampling cat-shaped, homemade ginger cookies from a blue floral earthenware platter.

"Sorry for not shaking hands," she apologized, surveying the yellow and blue stains on Leonora's white T-shirt, pants, and hands. She understood immediately.

"Oh my!" she groaned. "You must have been down to the Ludwig Factory. Blue and yellow are only two of the many horrid colorful—pardon the expression—substances at that toxic place. Acres bubbling with harmful chemical residue. We'd better take Peanut Butter to my vet immediately to clean her off properly," she added as she hurriedly reached for the phone to introduce the Wrights to the town veterinarian and warn him of their imminent arrival.

"And you, young lady, you must jump in the shower immediately. Wash yourself thoroughly, and dispose of your clothing. You can explain to your brother later . . ." Her voice trailed off as they ran out the door cat-in-the-bag. Quite an unusual—but understandable—monologue delivered hastily to the new residents.

Dr. Henry, the vet, was not in the least surprised by the sight of blue paws and a yellow underbelly. "Not the first time I've had to clean dangerous chemicals from a living creature," he mused sadly. "You're new in town, obviously, but we who live here know the sordid history of the place and stay as far away from there as we can," he continued after he had succeeded in removing every trace of the chemicals and shaved off the entire fur coat down to and including the last cat hair.

"Don't worry, she will be fine," he said, smiling reassuringly. "Thanks, Stacey. It's good that you brought them here quickly," he added as Peanut Butter shivered in his hands.

"Wow! Look at the bare skin. The calico colors and pattern are there," Laura pointed, cooing with delight.

"And her fur will fill in just fine again," Dr. Henry added. "Her coat will look the same. One of the wonders of nature. Amazing, isn't it?"

"But make sure you stay away from that polluted place, the above-ground sewer and eyesore of this town!" he cautioned in a solemn tone. "It is not safe for any human or animal!"

Back at the Wrights' kitchen table, tea resumed with the freshly showered, still traumatized Leonora joining. Stacey spoke with tightening lips, an undercurrent of anger in her tone: "That place has been empty and falling apart for years now, and the runoff from the metals which were used seeped into the ground and lagoon. A catastrophe! Didn't the real estate agent tell you about our 'problem'? That's an understated way to describe what is, in fact, our ongoing nightmare," she grumbled.

"No" was Laura's simple answer.

When the Wrights purchased their home, no one bothered to mention such a "problem." Shouldn't someone have been honest, you might wonder. The banker? The lawyer? The baker? The candlestick maker?

The Ludwig property was not on the same block, after all, so why bother? Perhaps the truth would have prevented the sale. Surely not the first time in human history that "Caveat emptor" ("Let the buyer beware") has been applicable. The Wrights had driven around the area and never thought twice about the old empty factory, not an uncommon sight in New England.

"The place is a giant chemical cesspool. A blight," Stacey elaborated. "A few of us have been fighting for years now to get Wigglesworth to clean it up. Such a shame: the good deed of old man Ludwig has been turned into a black mark on the soul of the area. A depository of poisons like arsenic and other chemicals. Turns my stomach just to think about it."

"What can be done?" Leonora asked innocently.

Since she was a little girl, Leonora had always been interested in science. It all began with a gift of a toy chemistry set. Then it continued early on at a Chinese restaurant where she was busily mixing salt, sugar, soy, sweet and sour, hot, and plum sauces with other condiments. She had been examining and mixing substances ever since. Girls of her generation were encouraged to become scientists, unlike the majority of their forbearers.

"We are just a handful of concerned citizens who are trying. Biffy Revere has been leading the charge and can tell you more. Her family lives closest to the site. She has had incredible stick-to-it-iveness, persistently working on trying to improve the situation. If you like, I can introduce you. Perhaps we can visit her tomorrow morning." And with three yeses in agreement and a quick call, a time was confirmed.

"Can we help?" Franz suggested with a youthful optimism not beaten down by decades of opposition and frustration. He, too, was a budding scientist interested in oceanography and hoping to be able to work at Woods Hole, a world-famous center nearby.

As he walked with his parents and sister along the marshes that evening, discussing the day's events, Will-o'-the-wisp lit the night air, and fireflies danced and darted across lawns. Poor Peanut Butter could only look out of the living room window; her tiny nose pressed to the glass. Campused: no trailing along on family walks for her for now.

"We'll find out tomorrow," Wolfgang said eagerly.

Chapter 4: A Day in the Life of Wigglesworth

When we first met him, it was Labor Day weekend, and Wigglesworth was grinning gleefully, lifting his right arm and snapping his fingers in the air as if they were a lobster's appendage.

"The claw is my motto, grabbing what I want," Wigglesworth snapped away, reminding his only daughter, Wilhelmina, as they strolled near his summer mansion in a wealthy seaside village a few miles away— he would not live in such a small, modest town as Ludwigshaven. He was joyously bringing her up to date on the string of lawsuits in which he had been embroiled, plus an exciting new one that he had initiated. Suing was one of his passions and entertainments.

"Always keep 'em off guard, at bay, on the run by suing," he chuckled, handing down his charming modus operandi to the next generation. "Like a deft sailor, wait for the winds to change, delay, about-face, try a new tack, create new moves, cry foul, and above all, avoid payment," he added, beaming with self-approbation.

"Always remember to keep a very low profile," he stressed, emphatically bending his knees momentarily as he lowered his head, tucking it partially into his T-shirt collar in a weird didactic demonstration.

Disputatious, one might call him. Quite a contrast to his beneficent, extroverted predecessor! Although Wigglesworth did not always win his suits, you can be sure he certainly tried every possible maneuver, especially waiting as long as he could to respond.

"Holding off makes 'em anxious and more likely to settle or do what I want," he explained to his chip-off-the-ol'-block, who was absorbing, admiring, and memorizing every precious word.

The latest? Earlier that day, in the case against his only brother, an innocent opponent, Wigglesworth had ordered his legal team: "Remain silent. Add time. Make sure his legal fees tabulate exponentially. Fun!"

And in the afternoon, he had launched a brand-new suit against his own mother-in-law! Her heinous crime? Her husband had died and left her, his beloved wife, his entire estate, to provide for her welfare—stipulating that their two children and son-in-law Wigglesworth would receive the proceeds when she passed on.

"How dare she!" Wigglesworth grumbled.

"What do you mean *she*?" queried his lawyer. "Her husband set it up that way."

"No, she wore the pants in that family. She influenced him to write the will as she wanted it. She will not get away with it," Wigglesworth responded, his face reddening with fury. "I'll fix her little wagon even if I have to eat up the estate in legal fees."

Clearly, Wigglesworth's crafty mind was concerned that the widow might use all the money before he could get his hands on it. To add a dollop of turmoil and provocation, he announced: "And let her know that her invitation to Wilhelmina's wedding has been rescinded."

"Her own—and only—granddaughter's upcoming very special day?" gulped the shocked attorney.

"Exactly," Wigglesworth said as he folded his arms across his chest and grinned.

"Anything more for today, Mr. W?" the lawyer asked. "It is Labor Day weekend, and my wife wants me to be with the family."

"I'll let you know if I think of anything. Always stand by. As usual," Wigglesworth answered in a cold, unfeeling tone.

"OK with you, Wilhelmina, dear?" Wigglesworth asked, reviewing his vengeful, bizarre strategy to the bride-to-be, who nodded in agreement. A cut from the same cloth. A true Wigglesworth-in-training, not in name only. With smiles of satisfaction on both faces, arms linked, they walked on.

"Everything will eventually belong to him, my daughter, and my grandchildren. Why is he suing me?" The aggrieved widow wept and cried in a call to a rational friend moments after hearing the news. "How could he do such things?"

There was no definitive answer except speculation about his self-proclaimed penchant for lawsuits and confirmation of his acquisitive nature.

"He is also involved in a suit with his own mother!" the friend reminded her.

A few mornings later, the day after Labor Day, Wigglesworth drove up to the decrepit old main gate of the factory. He had borrowed his lawyer's car rather than using his Mercedes, lest people notice his arrival in town—and partly to get free gas and reduce wear-and-tear on his own vehicle. Always calculating. . .

Sporting dark sunglasses and a baseball cap with an exceptionally large visor, he opened the driver's window to survey the scene, inspecting as the vehicle moved slowly along, hugging the curb near drooping fencing. One tour around the perimeter, and he drove off.

On his way out of town, he passed Leonora in front of her house, watching the back-to-work parade of cars. She was about to leave for her walk. He did not notice her, and she paid no special attention to him. Little did either suspect how their paths would cross again and what would ensue.

Chapter 5: Biffy's Saga

Stacey, Laura, Leonora, Franz, and Wolfgang joined Biffy once again on her porch.

"Wolfgang, that's an unusual name," Biffy queried as they chatted, getting to know one another.

"My mother loved music," Wolfgang answered. "Her family came from Austria, and she felt her only son should have the name of her hero, Mozart. I've certainly had my share of teasing when I was a kid. I was called the Wolf and many variations on a theme. But it's also been a plus, making me easily singled out and remembered."

"Well, the Wrights have come to the right place to learn more," Stacey began respectfully. "Biffy is a local hero to many here—and an enemy to others."

"I'm an old-timer," Biffy winked knowingly. "When you've lived long enough, you get to see a lot. Hackneyed but true, as most hackneyed statements are. But people do not dismiss hackneyed statements easily. Rather, they hang onto them because they usually contain profound meaning," she mused.

"Our long and short story is Wigglesworth," she intoned ominously. "William Wigglesworth."

"Some call him Wiggly," Stacey chimed in. "Piggy Wiggly. Or Wily Willy. There are lots of nicknames for him in this town. They should be burning his ears, but I suspect he may not know or would not care. I should think he would suspect by now how disliked he is. However . . ." She paused. "I wonder and doubt if his manipulative mind ever wanders to what we feel or if he has a shred of concern about the well-being of Ludwigshaven and its residents. There's no evidence of either."

"Wig-wart. The Worm," Stacey resumed, enumerating what was becoming a list.

"Please note that those are not terms of endearment, you can be sure," Biffy chuckled. "Scorn and derision are what he deserves and gets," she resumed her narrative with targeted focus, her voice rising. "Why, that man seems to be able to *wriggle* out of everything, wreck human lives, despoil the environment, and emerge seemingly unscathed! Ergo: Wriggly."

"Selfish, hateful, contemptible, a lowlife—common expressions fitting and befitting such a despicable person. Charles Dickens would probably have admired the singular appropriateness of his name!" Stacey added.

The Wrights leaned forward in their chairs, no longer leisurely rocking, feet now flat on the floor, listening intently.

"For decades, the factory machines were the engine of this town, roaring with energy, cranking up hopes, vibrating and pulsating to the satisfaction of contented families. And then came the new owner, Wig-wants, in his Mercedes Benz from Boston and took over the plant—until he ran it into the ground, literally and figuratively. One day, he suddenly closed the doors. Finished. Caput. Done."

"Why?" Franz and Leonora spoke simultaneously, looking baffled.

"Some say they were not keeping up with the competition," Stacey answered. "So they began to sell the machinery at first."

"Even when you know someone well, you cannot always comprehend what is in another mind," Biffy answered wistfully. "But a remote, aloof, uncommunicative stranger's motivations? Some speculate that he simply wanted to own a large tract of land as an investment. Maybe to build an estate? Housing? A shopping mall? Who knows? For years, the empty factory has simply remained closed."

Biffy stopped for a breath and continued, settling back in her chair. "Shutting down was just the start of his damaging activities. Over time, Wiggles*worthless* continued to live elsewhere while still owning the property here, and little by little, some of us began to understand the gravity of the situation. Residents were and are in danger, but he and his family were not," she sighed. "Approximately 7,200 people within a one-mile radius, 15,150 in a three-mile radius, an elementary school within 200 feet, 20 acres of tidal marsh contaminated by migration of hazardous substances. We tried to warn others. What a learning curve, and it is not over yet.

"We who live here continue to be affected, even if we don't wander into that property and prance through arsenic, yellow and blue runoff, not to mention a long laundry list of poisons. Runoff into the lagoon affects the fish, the marshes, the water. We need *all cleaned up*," Biffy spoke with intense emotion. "But Wigglesworth has evaded responsibility and accountability. Stonewalling. Failure to comply. No discussion. Nominal tidying up. Lawsuits and counter-lawsuits. Minimal communication. Doesn't answer the phone."

"How can that be?" Laura asked earnestly, mystified.

"A long and short story. In the mid-century, human beings around the world were slowly becoming aware of the shocking truth: we citizens, factories, industries, and governments had not been caring for and preserving our precious gifts, natural beauty, clean water, and the air we breathe. Rachel Cason was an early voice of science and reason in *Silent Spring*."

"Yes, her book is on our reading list at school this year," Leonora piped, "but I read it several years ago. She is one of my heroes—or heroines."

"Good to hear. Gradually, slowly, there has been growing awareness of the havoc wreaked in the name of progress, including dirty air, polluted waterways, and animals suffocating from unwanted items hurled carelessly and thoughtlessly into the sea," Biffy said, passionately charging ahead with her diatribe. "In

Ludwigshaven, the teachers understand. They have had frontline experience."

"But as you may know," Biffy said, "in some circles, *environmentalist* is a dirty word. There have been strong responses all over the world—*opposition* shouting the environmentalists down, hurling epithets, belittling them, skirting around increasing legislation. Oil rigs break down. Ships lose cargo and spread oil slicks for miles. Forests are denuded and destroyed. Neighborhood parks are replaced with skyscrapers, and on and on. It is, of course, not just a local issue. But our little town is a heinous example and sample, thanks to Piggy-Wiggly! We must work to maintain the sanctity of the land and the oceans."

"My ancestors were slaves, brought from Africa," Stacey spoke quietly, adding her perspective. "Bought and sold by calculating heartless business people. Our family made it up to the north. We have been here, free people, able to own land and work with pride. We didn't sign up for a new version of indifference and physical harm. We're proud homeowners in Ludwigshaven, and all of us—my husband, kids, and I—are on the posse out to get the offender and have the noxious ooze removed."

"Untreated wastewater at the factory has been discharged for years through leaky pipes," Stacey elaborated. "State officials reported site dangers and warned that animals and people—anyone and anything coming into contact with the area—would run an increased risk of health problems, cancer included. They demanded the company clean up, but Wigglesworth wiggled and wriggled. When the State sued, the company agreed to do some restoration and then 'fell behind in compliance.' Groundwater was potentially poisoning the lagoon."

"Here is a tip-of-the-iceberg timeline summary of the factory and property that we've made . . ." Pulling out a clipboard holding sheets of paper, she read aloud: "Here's the chronology . . .

"From the 1940s to the 1970s, Ludwig Factory's acids, metals, and solvents contaminated the soil, surface water, sediment, and ground water released into a lagoon near a marsh area.

"In the 1960s and 1970s, employees and townspeople noticed discoloration of soil and contamination, but they feared losing jobs and stayed silent.

"In the early 1980s, the state of Massachusetts demanded cleanup. Problem? Volatile organic compounds, arsenic, asbestos, and wastes containing cyanide, heavy metals, copper and nickel, polychlorinated biphenyls (PCBs), and acids.

"In small drinking water systems, research studies linked arsenic with cancer of the bladder, skin, kidney and non-cancerous conditions like high blood pressure and diabetes.

"As I told you, *egad*, approximately 7,200 people live within a one-mile radius, 15,000 in a three-mile radius. There is an elementary school within a few hundred feet, and 20 acres of tidal marsh were contaminated by the migration of hazardous substances. Wigglesworth does nothing.

"In 1982 and 1983, the state of Massachusetts sent notices to Ludwig Factory that groundwater is being poisoned by the lagoon. Ludwig Factory failed to respond.

"In 1984, the state of Massachusetts instituted a lawsuit against Ludwig Factory for violating pollution laws. Ludwig Factory agreed to clean up with a signed consent decree but fell behind in compliance.

"In 1985, the state of Massachusetts assumed control and hired a contractor to finish the cleanup of the lagoon.

"The State billed Ludwig Factory, which claimed that *the costs of cleanup were too high.*

"Ludwig Factory sued the State, the contractor, and its own insurer, who refused to pay $500,000 to $1,000,000 for the cleanup. Ludwig Factory lost every case and was supposed to pay most of the bill.

"In 1985, Ludwig Factory closed and was not properly maintained. Broken windows and deteriorating buildings potentially released asbestos into the environment.

"In 1990, Ludwig Factory was placed on the Superslime Project.

"In 1992, the Super Environmental Agency (SEA) announced the Administrative Record File on Ludwig Factory and encouraged the public to review and comment on it.

"The first administrative order was issued, and the potentially responsible party, William Wigglesworth, was to conduct removal activities.

"The second administrative order was issued, and the potentially responsible party, William Wigglesworth, failed to comply.

"In 1998, a feasibility study was done by SEA.

"In 1999, Wigglesworth failed to comply.

"In 1999, the town sued Ludwig Factory to force demolition of a building and to remove asbestos. Visible asbestos and pipes with carcinogenic materials in other buildings were left in place. Broken windows and deteriorating buildings released asbestos fibers into the air and were an inhalation risk to the community. **Exposure to asbestos is associated with asbestosis, a chronic, debilitating lung disease, and is also linked to the development of mesothelioma, a form of cancer.**

"The area remained contaminated with poisonous materials known to cause cancer and other illnesses. Anyone or anything coming into contact with the area could be in danger.

"The SEA administrator declared in a press release: 'They have been a problem since day one. Ludwig Factory has declared it would not undertake removal. Since they are refusing to comply with the order, our number-one priority is the safety of the community. Unfortunately, Ludwig Factory doesn't seem to share this priority. Therefore, we will begin to remove asbestos-containing materials at the site.'

"Ludwig Factory argued that the government studies were flawed and the property should never have been listed on the Superslime Project.

"Complaining the tests were only conducted in most polluted areas and never proving anything measured above the approved levels, Ludwig Factory argued that *the government would be wasting taxpayer time and money to go ahead with the cleanup.*

"You see. This has been going on for *years*! There is still a lot of work to be done," Biffy resumed. "The dilapidated buildings are a fire hazard and need to be demolished. The land around them is filled with dangerous poisons. The town is owed more than $180,000 in back taxes and interest."

"And the gall to argue that he is trying to save the taxpayers money!" Biffy laughed. "It is almost comical! And take a look at this excerpt from a deposition:"

Volume 1

Pages 1 to 110

Exhibits 1 to 19

UNITED STATES DISTRICT COURT

Excerpt from:

DISTRICT OF MASSACHUSETTS

- - - - - - - - - - - x

UNITED STATES OF AMERICA,:   Civil Action

Plaintiff

vs.

LUDWIG FACTORY and: with Lead Cause

WILLIAM WIGGLESWORTH,   for Discovery

Defendants . . . Only

DEPOSITION OF WILLIAM WIGGLESWORTH, a witness called on behalf of the United States of America

DIRECT EXAMINATION

Q. Mr. Wigglesworth, do you understand that you are under oath?

A. I do.

Q. How often do you visit the Ludwig Factory?

A. Once a week.

Q. Do you have an office in the building?

A. No, I visit the offices of the employees running the factory.

Q. Have you ever noticed blue or yellow runoff on the grounds?

A. No.

Q. Have you ever seen chemicals being expelled into the lagoon?

A. No.

Meanwhile, Laura had turned ashen white during the reading.

"I am absolutely shocked," she began slowly, searching for the words to express her dismay. "Simply horrified," she said and paused momentarily. "I had heard and read about Superslime locations in the country, but I had no idea our lives would be inextricably intertwined with one."

The silence was dramatic; no one moved, not even a facial muscle.

"In this great country?" Laura cried. "Veritable poisoning going relatively unchecked for decades? We the people," she continued. "We are responsible for each other and our country! Desecrate this land? Literally? Harm others?"

"When I think of my grandparents, immigrants from Eastern Europe, fleeing from pogroms and starvation . . ." Laura's cheeks reddened as she spoke. "The United States, to them, was a land of promise and goodness. Such abundance that stories circulated about money growing on trees here. My father was grateful for the safety, chance, and privilege to be an American and taught us to be thankful for every opportunity, to give charity, to help our fellow man.

"He was proud of his citizenship. Loyalty to our flag and to this great democracy was fundamental to his everyday existence. He would have been horrified, too. He reared us to protect the greatest treasures we have been given, and freedom is high on the list. Freedom to do positive things, not negative nor destructive."

"You are an idealist and a very positive person," Wolfgang said to her as he gently took her hand and patted it soothingly. "We cannot be naive. We know about human nature and evil. We are not naive. I recently read a report about the state of Maine, where one hundred different locations had their water systems at unacceptable drinking levels.

"We are all very privileged and lucky to be in this great country of ours and very fortunate to live under the rule of law," he continued. "There is legislation to protect the environment and public servants, including legislators and judges, to reinforce what is required. The Super Environmental Agency is an amazing creation, but it has an enormous task or series of tasks. The government and the legal system often move turtle-fashion, slowly. Our job is to stand up for what is right, obviously, wherever and whenever necessary."

"Have you tried to draw national attention to this dilemma?" Wolfgang turned back to Biffy and Stacey.

"We've just moved from Washington, where I have been writing as a journalist, and I know members of Congress from Massachusetts and others who might help. Another great aspect of our country is freedom of the press, and I'm ready to exercise that right, to use it to the fullest."

Little did Biffy and Stacey know that fate had brought them an ideal audience, scientifically oriented and loaded with the power of the pen—i.e., both a journalist and an artist who was known for her children's drawing style.

"We have to explore every possibility," Biffy responded with delight. "Up to now, we've done all we know how to do to inform the public, badger local journalists, and hold meetings. We've been social warriors on a tiny turf. Let me show you. Please follow me into my study."

Rising abruptly, the four Wrights and Stacey trailed after her, through a formal living room with portraits of ancestors on the walls, past the mahogany table, chairs, and sideboard of the dining room, beyond a spacious old-fashioned kitchen, to a bookcase-lined nook behind white louvered doors.

"Here are some of the local newspaper reports." She pointed up above her desk to side-by-side bulletin boards tacked with bold headlines of yellowing articles from the *Ludwigshaven Gazette.*

All eyes were fixed, reading:

> Wigglesworth Remains Silent
> Wigglesworth Refuses to Answer Questions
> Toxic Wasteland Has Indifferent Owner
> State Officials Arrive Today to Inspect Wasteland
> Wigglesworth's Attorney Delays Court Hearing
> Wigglesworth Postpones Another Court Date
> Marshland Toxins
> Tainted Ground Water
> Fishermen Meet in Protest with Huge Outcry
> Birds Found Dead Floating among the Marsh Grasses

Wigglesworth Refuses to Cooperate with the
Government
A Thorn in Ludwigshaven's Side: Roof Collapse
Just Latest Problem
Ludwigshaven Counsel: Talks Have Broken
Down

"And here are more," Biffy added, opening a deep drawer in a tall white filing cabinet. "The culprit has ingeniously toyed with local authorities and been consistently uncooperative. Wigglesworth tactics 101: ignore, delay, and be unavailable. Look at these files, if you like, and at these scrapbooks with additional articles and reports. A local TV reporter interviewed me and made a video just a few weeks ago," she added, pointing to a monitor, "if you'd like to watch it. A heart-broken local resident tells her story, and I do too."

"A big underlying issue is controlling runoff from stormwater transporting pollutants like oil, grease, toxic chemicals, pesticides, and bacteria. These waters are vital to our drinking water needs, wildlife, and recreation," Stacey adds.

"The result: nothing much happens. Here and there, someone stirs, but the situation has not changed in any significant way," Biffy says summarily.

"Of course! But what you—or we—need is news coverage and help beyond the town," Wolfgang pressed on with enthusiasm. "Ludwigshaven is a *very* unusual place, with a potentially *very* interesting story. How many small towns are there in the entire world where a local boy returns home with the enormous financial success of a magnate like Charles Ludwig? One who then chooses not only to revitalizes the economy but also to fund such a quantity and variety of municipal buildings and parks? And a close friend of Mark Twain, one of the nation's greatest writers and minds?

"At the very least, an interesting, inspiring tale of generosity, loyalty, kindness, and caring," he emphasized. "A heart-warming story in itself, too. But add to that the new twist, a modern-day scrooge with a slew of unredeemable qualities. Contrast the profiles and characteristics of Ludwig versus Wigglesworth, top it off with a battle for the environment, and you have a lollapalooza of an attention-getting news story. But of course, I need to know more."

"Whenever you are ready to begin," Biffy's expression changed in an instant from grim to grin. "Have I got news and history for you."

"How about a break for lunch, and we can return this afternoon," Wolfgang suggested. "No time like the present to get started. And let's begin with as much information on Wigglesworth as possible—and what makes him tick. I need to analyze the facts in order to understand what we are up against and what may be the next steps."

"Great! Thank *you*! We are just a small band of citizens doing whatever we could think of." Stacey clasped her hands together with joy, proud to have been the go-between who produced a potentially surprising outcome. "How wonderful it would be if we, just a dot in the universe, one small spot in our great country, could have the success and impact we need."

Chapter 6: Celebrations and Testimony by Deep Throat

Gathering again on Biffy's porch, the four newcomers and two old-timers settled into their respective chairs with anticipation and curiosity.

"Some town history for background and perspective first," Biffy announced, opening a scrapbook filled with photographs.

"A new way to measure time," she joked. "I call it BW. Before Wigglesworth. Look here. In Mr. Ludwig's lifetime, the factory grounds were always a hub of activity and productivity, including people having fun, clambakes, and Christmas parties. What is now a wasteland was the scene of many memorable, special celebrations where we, the local citizens, gathered at his invitation.

"July Fourth was one of the highlights. *Everyone* went to the annual morning parade that began at the library and ended up at the Ludwig Factory. Why, the sounds of trumpets, trombones, flutes, clarinets, and glockenspiel literally shattered the air"—she flipped through the pages, pointing and smiling—"as the high school band marched in orange-and-black uniforms to the beat of snare and bass drums.

Why do I say *shattered*?" Biffy stopped and had a mischievous look as she asked. "Well, any and all local folks who could play an instrument could join, no matter what level of expertise, so you can imagine! The only criteria were enthusiasm and willingness to attend rehearsals. A community effort, a New England tradition.

"The factory grounds were dotted with picnic tables and folding chairs. Red, white, and blue cloths decorated long buffets topped with children's dream menus: heaping platters of juicy hot dogs, soft buns, sizzling hamburgers, peanut-butter-and-jelly sandwiches, French fries, ketchup, mustard, sodas, and juices.

"Plus fresh-caught lobsters, corn on the cob, and coleslaw for differing taste buds. An all-you-could-eat American picnic: platters brimming with piles of rich chocolate brownies, red-white-and-blue flag cookies, and cupcakes slathered with scrumptious red, white, and blue icing. Red, white and blue paper napkins and stove-pipe paper hats were given to all. Games, relay races, square dancing—and the band played on. Long sultry afternoons idled away in summer activities." She paused to hand around additional scrapbooks from a pile on a side table.

"Every person—big, small, short, tall, newborn, or centenarian—went home with a gift basket of fruit and sweets. I remember Mr. Ludwig handing them out to all, shaking hands, making conversation. He never missed a year. We celebrated until he passed away," she resumed, wiping a tear from her eye.

"And what happened if it rained?" asked Franz, who was into comfort.

"No expense was spared. The recreation hall was decorated, and tents, tents, and more tents—large white tents like the Arabian nights—erected for the occasion," Biffy's blue eyes sparkled, and her face lit up at the thought of them.

"Mind you—the July Fourth celebrations were simply outdone by Thanksgiving, Mr. Ludwig's favorite holiday. Football games, parades, more marching band cacophony, buffets with juicy turkey, sweet potato, cornbread, and all the fixings—including cranberry sauce from bogs growing not far from here—pumpkin and pecan pies, apple cider, steaming hot chocolate, and a chocolate turkey for each guest. Decorations in autumn colors: cloths, plates, and napkins in shades of yellow, orange, and brown. Ending with cornucopia-shaped straw baskets loaded with candy and turkey-shaped cookies to take home. Year after year, handed individually to each person by Mr. Ludwig himself. We had a great deal to be thankful for in those good old days," she said wistfully.

"And we still do, but . . ." As she paused, her shoulders sank.

"Thanksgiving is my favorite holiday, too," Leonora jumped in to fill the silence. "I love it. A day set aside for all Americans, no matter what religion or background. We all gather and remember how the early settlers gave thanks for their survival and lives in the New World. Thinking about the Pilgrims is very inspiring to me, especially now that we are living here, not far from where they settled."

"We will take you over to the Plimouth Plantation one day, and not far from there, you can see a replica of what people think the Mayflower was like. Can you imagine how this area looked then?" Biffy asked, and without taking a breath, proceeded to answer her own question.

"Canoes swishing through the marshes, Indians helping the newcomers to plant corn, communities being built, emigres enduring winter hardships in a new environment. Sounds romantic in retrospect, and oversimplified, of course, but they were forging a new country, where one day Thomas Jefferson would write: 'All men are created equal.' Earthshaking in the history of the Western world. Truly a *new world* in many senses and the beginning of one of the rare human experiments, a long-lasting and thriving democracy. Imperfect, riddled with inconsistencies, but improving, aiming toward 'a more perfect union.'"

"In his account, Governor Bradford complained that he and his fellow Puritans were bored eating a diet consisting mainly of lobsters. Sounds strange to us today," Leonora added.

"Such an expensive delicacy and treat nowadays draws tourists swarming to New England every summer," Biffy responded. "Lobsters were plentiful and commonplace for the early settlers. But not much else. Many did not survive that first winter. They didn't have the benefits of our modern agriculture and our plentiful tables but were lucky to have Native Americans teaching them how to plant corn and other food suitable to these parts. It's all relative. Yes, times have changed, for sure."

There are many ways to look back on that history, dear reader, and many conflicting points of view, but please be patient. Slavery and mistreatment of Native Americans will be factored in and discussed later in our story.

"Changed for us, too, especially AW," Stacey lowered her voice and half-covered her mouth as if sharing a secret, "another way of measuring time, our code for *After Wigglesworth*'s arrival on the scene."

"Since 1620, around here, humans have found numerous ways to mar the landscape over the centuries," Biffy the elder, the philosopher-queen of Ludwigshaven, continued her musings. "And now, AW, we have our task to rectify the damage, including and starting right here in our little town. We who have been graced with an uncaring, defiant Wigglesworth. With him, our lives were altered, and Ludwig Factory celebratory holidays—especially our unique, privileged, marvelous Thanksgivings—ended."

"In short, *nothing* from Wigglesworth at first, and then *nothing but trouble*," Stacey exclaimed. "Ten cheerless acres with rotting buildings and quietly seeping chemicals. Bubble, bubble, toil and trouble."

"What else do you know about him?" Wolfgang asked, ready to take notes. "What about those stories you mentioned? The more we understand about him, the better, obviously."

"Bottom line: money, money, money!" Biffy exclaimed. "According to our sources, he rises in his pursuit, spends the day in the chase, and goes to bed to dream of more, more, more. From dawn to dusk, the king is in his counting house counting out his money. Tight-fisted, unwilling to spend a dime without turning it over ten times, as they say—or a hundred times, in his case. I believe that if you held a stethoscope to his chest, you would hear 'Hold on tight; never let it go' from his core, a pulsating inner refrain rather than a normal heartbeat!"

"He has a company in Boston, Big Deals Industries. The address is a small three-story narrow brownstone he owns. A tax return he filed claimed 260 employees *at that location*, surely a physical impossibility in that little space," Stacey proceeded. "It makes no sense. When you call, if anyone bothers to answer, a voice simply says, 'Hello.' No company name. Wigglesworth is never available, always in meetings. Never returns calls."

"Odd," Wolfgang noted. "Or a fabrication? A headquarters? Are there other companies? Or a front?"

The journalist was now taking notes rapidly, asking question after question.

"Where does he live?"

"One home is in the best section of historic Beacon Hill. Another is a waterfront mansion with eleven bedrooms, a private beach, and a guest cottage in Cape Cod. You can see it from a boat if we take you for a sail," Biffy explained.

"That's where our two Deep Throats come in," Biffy laughed heartily. "Sherlock One and Two, to mix metaphors!"

"You have to be kidding!" Wolfgang retorted with amusement.

"No kidding! We have two veritable first-hand witnesses who have taped their observations, which I loosely call testimony," Biffy answered seriously. "Insight into his character, for whatever it is worth."

"The Washington boys, George and Ben—they live over on Samoset. One summer, Wigglesworth hired them to paint the entire exterior and interior of his house, as well as the guest cottage where he put them up. So they were there day and night, watching and listening. Very smart kids, reliable and trustworthy," Stacey explained. "What they have to report gives quite a bit of insight into the character—or lack of one—of our dear Wiggles*worth-less*."

"The boys saw and heard a *lot* that summer, starting with Wigglesworth's demonstration of his 'claw,'" Biffy continued, "his self-proclaimed motto. He calls it a visual symbol of how he operates. Apparently, he waves his hand in the air, grabbing and snapping. Probably singularly appropriate here in lobster country!" she snickered.

"More detail?" Wolfgang asked. Curious, curious, curiouser.

"Their penny-pinching employer paid a bargain hourly rate, but the boys were happy to have a summer job. Day by day, their big boss commuted to and from Boston. Each evening, he returned with exactly the number of cans of paint required to continue for the next day. Instead of buying a case, he doled out, drop by drop, never wanting to spend a cent more than necessary at the moment. The words *tightwad* and *skinflint* come to mind," Biffy added with a modicum of sarcasm.

"Or control freak," Stacey speculated and suggested.

"We decided to tape the boys' testimony, especially since they are off to college and not always available," said Biffy, turning on a recording. "Here, listen to George's own words."

"He bragged to us about his real estate and other 'deals,'" a booming basso voice on the tape resounded.

"That's George," Stacey explained. "He sings in the choir. Can't miss that gorgeous vocal quality."

"A lonely guy, that Mr. Wigglesworth. Told us over and over 'how lonely it is at the top,'" George on tape went on. "Sometimes, he tried to joke around with us. He repeatedly talked about his 'sense of hummah,' but he is *not* very funny."

"Like a gorilla thumping on his chest, he was really proud of buying that enormous house," George on tape continued. "He bragged about turning a small investment into what he called a one-of-a-kind acquisition. Repeatedly, he relished telling us about his discovery of an ad in the local paper, listing a huge old house donated to a church in a congregant's will."

"'The church was dying to get rid of the place, and I *snapped* it up at a bargain price of $100,000,' Wigglesworth told us. Sounds like a lot? Shrewdly and craftily, he sold a small beach house that had cost him $30,000 and had risen in value to $100,000. Then he plowed the proceeds of the sale into the run-down waterfront property soon worth millions, especially thanks to our superb paint job!"

"Clever, one must admit," Biffy commented. "Do not underestimate him."

"As Labor Day rolled around," Ben on tape explained, "we had not completed the massive painting task, although we worked seven days a week from early morning to sunset. It was time for us to go back to Harvard, but Wiggy roared, threatened, and insisted that we stay until every inch had been painted. He was fuming, snarling over and over about how lucky we had been to have a summer vacation at a private beach. That's how he described our close-to-indentured-servant labor. We were terrified by his unreasonable demands, and we had to get our parents to intervene and help us get out of there."

"*A man of business* to the gills, with a business mind and skills," Biffy the Rhymester intoned, "but what about the human side? Their encounter is the tip of the proverbial iceberg as far as his interaction with people."

"And the boys are just getting started," said Biffy, turning on the recording again.

"He always waited until his car was riding near empty, on its last gallon, before refilling. Sundays were often a mad dash. When most gas stations were closed, he would be hunting for fuel for miles and barely making it to a place that was open. Usually, he had only fifty cents in his pocket. Quite hard on himself even though he had a big bank account," Ben on tape observed.

"I remember the first time he lost his tennis match. He was depressed for several days. He *could not* bear to lose. It would make him literally sick and dysfunctional. He would repeat over and over, reviewing the game. Very strange," George on tape was speaking.

"And then there were his lawsuits," Ben on tape intervened. "That guy *loves* to sue. Fun and games for him. He happily repeated what he called his basic strategies: don't respond, keep people waiting, delay, push the adversary around, stall, and much more.

"While suing his mother-in-law, he was also suing his only brother and his own mother—for almost a decade. Why? Vendettas. Different reasons for different people. In the case of his mother, he was angry his father had not left him in charge, a trustee of his mother's estate. The case dragged on like another *Bleak House,* and he happily inflicted emotional turmoil on the family. The result? No change. Who benefitted? Lawyers in pairs charging hundreds of thousands of dollars, but ongoing conflict and nuisance value were very precious to dear Will. You should have heard him talk, recounting details like a warrior in battle.

"One night, he and Wilhelmina went for a walk," George on tape continued the narrative. "Her younger brother distanced himself and had nothing to do with them. But she is a lot like her dear father. They work together. When they returned, they told us about hearing a neighbor's sons arguing with and screaming at their mother.

"'The father never intervenes when they scream or even when the boys beat their mother,' Wigglesworth pointed out. 'He enables and allows them to do *what he would like to do*. Through them, he expresses his rage and anger.'"

"Can you imagine?" Ben on tape concluded with horror. "The father/husband they were analyzing was *Wigglesworth's closest and only friend*."

"My mother used to say: 'Show me who your friends are, and I will show you who you are,'" Biffy remarked. "That little evening lesson about human psychology and relationships is quite illuminating, to say the least."

"Another favorite topic was his art collection and how he was buying for investment," George on tape explained. "Not a word about the love of art! He had a strategy in that arena too: 'Bargain with the artist to beat the price down to the lowest conceivable number and insist the artist personally deliver the work from another state, from miles away, wherever . . . and then to arrange to send monthly installments of $25 or $50, dragging out payment for *years*,' he told us."

"Quite a fellow," Laura commented, feeling sympathy for her fellow artists who had to deal with such an endearing *patron*.

"Wow!" Wolfgang exclaimed, gathered his notes, and stood up abruptly. "You've certainly given us a lot of information. I'd like to think about all we've discussed and get back to you."

The meeting adjourned, and the participants went to their respective corners and daily lives.

Chapter 7: Action

Within days, and with the full approval and participation of Biffy and Stacey, the Wrights went into action to right the wrongs, so to speak, each using his or her special skills. As a six-member self-proclaimed Wright-the-Wrongs team, they devised a plan and began to pursue their goals with frequent discussions and flexible implementation. All agreed to focus first on drawing public attention to Ludwigshaven's environmental plight as a crucial step to altering what they revealed in calling the *Wigglesworth-slime situation*.

Had the stars aligned? Had fate indeed deposited *the* family perfectly suited to aid in the task in the tiny town? One can only speculate on when, why, and how change occurs, but the results were simply astonishing to Biffy and Stacey, who had worried and agonized for years.

Wolfgang contacted his vast array of friends in Washington, and within weeks, not one but two US senators from Massachusetts appeared on Biffy's doorstep, asking questions and offering help and support.

"My staff and I will now be working with local officials and Ludwigshaven citizens to implement a cleanup plan," proclaimed Senator Bernie Frankel, a well-known, respected Harvard-trained lawyer and activist. "We will hold public meetings to ensure community involvement and to answer questions. This is an example of why I support an adequately funded government to take care of such projects that require money. SEA has stabilized conditions that pose an imminent risk to the community by removing asbestos-containing materials."

"We have come to see with our own eyes, and it is an eyesore," Senator Holly Putnam added. "As a wife and mother, I must remind everyone that there is a school several hundred feet away. We are pleased to make sure that initial community concerns will be accommodated by SEA. We cannot tolerate another moment of damage to the ecology of our magnificent bay. You have my support and attention. Don't hesitate to contact me about whatever you need."

Their interviews were carried on local and national radio and TV in wire services and newspapers, flooding the networks and the newsstands. Accompanied, of course, by graphic images from the Ludwig Factory grounds, stories told by distraught local residents, and explanations about the composition and consequences of the specific harmful chemicals. Wolfgang's writing and journalistic contacts were serving them well and keeping him very busy.

Biffy was particularly cheered and proud to be photographed with Stacey and the two legendary titans from Congress—standing defiantly, no less, right under the "Ludwig Factory: DO NOT ENTER" sign. What an honor! How amused they also seemed to be, as the four linked arms for another picture near a new sign that had recently mysteriously appeared—thanks to Wigglesworth—on the fencing: "ATTACK DOG: KEEP OUT!"

Laura's drawings and cartoons illustrating and satirizing Wigglesworth and his haunting, poisonous, disturbing site were companion pieces for the informative texts. Here are the first three in a long line of her inspired creations:

BEFORE: The Garden of Eden, Plimouth (1620),
a scene of natural beauty

AFTER: Wigglesworth in the Garden

Laura has drawn the same scene, dominated by a large slithering snake with the head of the devil surrounded by bubbling fluids.

Sue, Sue, Just-suits Shall Ye Pursue.

Laura drew a towering Uncle Sam holding Blind Justice on his arm, shouting triumphantly down on a small Wigglesworth, who uses both hands and elbows out to block his ears.

Win Best Nickname Contest.

A hand is about to pick the winning name from a large glass bowl of entries (handwritten on paper) as a crowd looks on.

- Wiggly
- Wriggly
- Piggy Wiggly
- Wily Willy

- Wig-wart
- The Worm
- Wig-wants
- The Wily One
- Wiggle*worth-less*
- Wiggle-swamp

At school, Leonora and Franz, the new kids on the block, were becoming quite the hit. *Everyone* wanted to get to know them, talk to them before, in, and after classes, and walk home with them—even if it took one a mile or two out of the way. The twins joined the Science Club and made many new friends who cared about the environment in general and, in particular, the local issues confronting Ludwigshaven.

Under Laura's and Wolfgang's guidance, they enlisted fellow students to write hundreds of letters to state representatives, congressmen and congresswomen, and government officials, describing their plight and asking for assistance.

Mr. Newton, the science teacher, gave Leonora, Franz, and other chemistry students a detailed analysis of the putrid substances emanating from the factory grounds and a new, special series of classes on protecting the environment.

He shepherded a new afterschool club, Saving the Planet, which offered varied activities and trips, hosted guest speakers, and did fund-raising to educate students and heighten awareness of ecology, alternative energy sources, and cutting-edge developments. Little by little, the endangered residents were learning the details and extent of their very own local pollution.

The school paper, *The Never Missbehaven*, created a new front-page segment, Lifting the Lid, dedicated to uncovering the latest news and developments in the Ludwig Factory story. Leonora, Franz, and many others wrote extensive articles that were often reprinted in the national press and beamed across wire services.

A consortium of scientists visited to analyze the dangerous chemicals oozing within a one-mile radius and issued the following eye-popping and mind-bending list with a colorful chart of circles representing:

- ALDRIN
- CHROMIUM
- DIELDRIN
- COPPER
- BENZO[A]ANTHRACENE
- CYANIDE
- 2-CHLOROPHENOL
- ACENAPHTHYLENE
- BIS(2-CHLOROISOPROPYL) ETHER
- SILVER
- BENZOIC ACID
- 2-METHYLPHENOL (O-CRESOL)
- AROCLOR 1260
- BENZO(B)FLUORANTHENE
- BARIUM

- COBALT
- CYANIDE
- XYLENE (MIXED ISOMERS)
- CADMIUM
- ARSENIC
- COPPER
- NICKEL
- ZINC
- BENZO[A]ANTHRACENE
- BENZO(K)FLUORANTHENE
- BIS(2-ETHYLHEXYL)PHTHALATE
- DI-N-OCTYL PHTHALATE
- MERCURY
- NAPHTHALENE
- PHENYLMETHANOL
- P,P'-DDT
- BENZO(K)FLUORANTHENE
- COPPER
- DIBENZO(A,H)ANTHRACENE
- PHENANTHRENE
- LEAD
- 1,2-DIHYDROACENAPHTHYLENE
- BIS(2-ETHYLHEXYL)PHTHALATE
- DIBUTYL PHTHALATE
- MANGANESE
- CHRYSENE
- INDENO(1,2,3-CD)PYRENE
- CHROMIUM
- ETHYLBENZENE

- CHLOROMETHANE
- P,P'-DDD
- ALUMINUM
- VANADIUM
- BENZO[A]PYRENE
- CHRYSENE
- DIETHYL PHTHALATE
- ZINC
- P,P'-DDE
- P,P'-DDT
- ACENAPHTHYLENE
- ALUMINUM
- ANTIMONY
- DIBENZOFURAN
- GAMMA-HEXACHLOROCYCLOHEXANE (LINDANE)
- 2-METHYLNAPHTHALENE
- BIS(2-ETHYLHEXYL)PHTHALATE
- BENZO(B)FLUORANTHENE
- MANGANESE
- 1,3-DICHLOROBENZENE
- 1,4-DICHLOROBENZENE
- 4-(4-AMINO-3-CHLOROPHENYL)-2-CHLOROANILINE
- 4-NITROPHENOL
- ANTHRACENE
- BARIUM
- DIMETHYL PHTHALATE

- 2-METHYLNAPHTHALENE
- BENZO[A]PYRENE
- BENZO(GHI)PERYLENE
- BETA-HEXACHLOROCYCLOHEXANE
- PYRENE
- VANADIUM
- ALUMINUM
- BENZENE
- BERYLLIUM COMPOUNDS
- ANTIMONY
- DIBENZO(A,H)ANTHRACENE
- 2,4-DINITROTOLUENE
- BUTYL BENZYL PHTHALATE
- HEXACHLORO-1,3-BUTADIENE
- 3,5,5-TRIMETHYLCYCLOHEX-2-EN-1-ONE
- PHENANTHRENE
- BUTYL BENZYL PHTHALATE
- DICHLOROMETHANE (METHYLENE CHLORIDE)
- 2-METHYLPHENOL (O-CRESOL)
- NAPHTHALENE
- VANADIUM
- 2-METHYLNAPHTHALENE
- BERYLLIUM
- CHRYSENE
- NAPHTHALENE
- MANGANESE
- TOLUENE

- 2-METHYLPHENOL (O-CRESOL)
- 4-METHYLPHENOL (P-CRESOL)
- CHROMIUM
- INDENO(1,2,3-CD)PYRENE
- 2-CHLORONAPHTHALENE
- 2-NITROPHENOL
- PENTACHLOROPHENOL

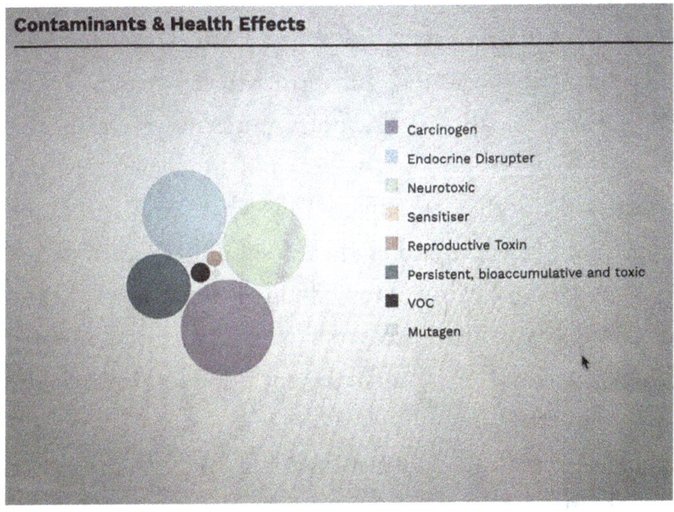

Mr. Newton posted the information in his classroom, in the hall of the school, and in leaflets distributed by hand:

- Carcinogen
- Endocrine Disrupter
- Neurotoxic
- Sensitiser

- Reproductive Toxin
- Persistent, bioaccumulative and toxic
- VOC
- Mutagen

"Studying those lists would surely keep Mr. Newton and his science classes busy for more than a semester!" Wolfgang wrote in a comprehensive article relating to specific scientific research on each item.

"Cyanide, arsenic, mercury, lead—if you don't recognize these names," he addressed his readers, "it is high time we all do. We must understand the health risks: what is in our air, water, and food and how our minds and bodies are affected by what we breathe and consume. 'Educate and eradicate' should be our motto."

Indeed, Mr. Newton divided up the lists and assigned his students research papers and oral reports. They discussed the high concentration of metals and PCBs in the water and sediment. There were more than 142 entries of contaminants of concern to human health and to the ecology in groundwater, soil, sediment, buildings, runoff, and air. Egad!

Leading professors from prestigious universities—great experts—were invited by the town official to give talks to families on special evenings in the high school auditorium. One summarized a report done by a colleague: "People living and working nearby are potentially exposed to PCBs through contact with water and sediments in the indoor air and indoor dust and consumption of seafood caught from the harbor. Cancer risks associated with seafood consumption are relatively well-characterized and have been the basis for closures of areas to fishing and fish consumption."

He spoke about the "PCBs volatilized (present in the gas phase) or aerosolized (suspended in water droplets or with particulate matter) into the surrounding air" and warned of "residential exposures and health risk for residents and risk from consumption of contaminated fish and shellfish and inhalation of the air as well as changes in thyroid hormone levels in infants, children, and adults as a function of exposure. Thyroid hormones are essential for normal behavioral, intellectual, and neurologic development, and inadequate levels of these hormones have a negative effect on brain development."

Moans and groans were heard punctuating his narrative from concerned members of the audience. They agreed to participate in hosting air samples on their properties, testing, analysis, and community engagement methods—whatever would help to understand the dangers they were facing.

He suggested a list of studies to read, including the following:

- Consumption of contaminated seafood
- Prenatal and postnatal exposure to persistent organic pollutants and attention-deficit and hyperactivity disorder

- Endocrine-disrupting chemicals: effects on neuroendocrine systems and the neurobiology of social behavior
- Thyroid-disrupting chemicals
- Increased risk of diabetes and polychlorinated biphenyls and dioxins
- Polychlorinated biphenyl serum levels, thyroid hormones, and endocrine and metabolic diseases in people living in a highly polluted area

Chapter 8: News

As the story of Ludwigshaven's history and environmental battle spread, the worldwide press swarmed into town. They flocked to watch and laud young people, the next generation, preparing for the future, caring for the planet, working together with their families and townspeople to protect the earth. Fodder for hundreds of news stories.

"All unfolding near the very place where a ragged bunch of hopeful, tired, and weary Pilgrims long ago sought freedom and established a new civilization on this side of the Atlantic," one journalist waxed poetic. "Historic, important, a thread from the past to the present. Where settlers solemnly and joyously paused to be *thankful*, once again where it all began. Something, much, in fact, to be VERY *thankful* for."

And soon, *thankful* became the keyword, the tagline, inextricably linked with the evolving saga.

The town fathers and mothers were simply delighted by the turn of events and the attention. Concerned about how to best represent all aspects of the issue, contests were announced. The one that elicited the widest response was the following:

MOST CREATIVE DESCRIPTION OF LUDWIGSHAVEN
Categories: drawing, painting, photography, literary

Households were abuzz with children of all ages, as well as adults, immersed in watercolors, crayons, cameras, drawing paper, and writing. The entries were the subject of press coverage, transmitted rapidly to the world at large.

Wolfgang had been correct: what a story! People across the country and the globe warmed to the idea of the longevity and quality of Mr. Ludwig's generosity. And their hackles were raised at the very thought of blue paws, contaminants with adverse, unfavorable side effects, and dangerous indifference to human suffering.

A folk tale with real *folk*. A narrative with living, engaged narrators. A chronicle of successes and failures. A story of commitment to ideals. And it wasn't over.

"There is a lot to be done," tireless Biffy told a flock of reporters who trailed her every move on a tour of the town and its infamous, now-growing-famous eyesore.

"Such a 10-acre super-sewer cannot be transformed overnight despite all the collaborative efforts," she explained. "Meetings are being held, calls made and followed up, and pressure applied in every way known."

The fire chief held a news conference of his own to discuss his alarm and concerns about the possibility of fires or explosions on the Ludwig Factory property.

"We are *thankful* that nothing so dramatic has occurred, but we are wary and cautious. Recently, a roof on the property collapsed," he explained.

"The fire department will no longer enter the building. There are safety and ignition risks: lightning or arson. The caretaker was notified and will notify the owners—that is, the Ludwig Factory in care of Big Deals Industries. Currently, $500,000 in back taxes are owed."

As Ludwigshaven-watching caught on, the media also camped out near Wigglesworth's properties to capture a glimpse or snapshot of the notorious litigant and withholding owner. Sequestered, invisible, he stayed out of sight and refused to speak or respond to anyone interested. Nowhere to be seen. Not a trail, not a track. Not even a footprint on his private beach.

"He might have joined the wave of humanity, admitted his failures, and tried to rectify his wrongs," Laura suggested. "We've read of numerous other Superslime Projects where the owners have done just that (or tried to), contributed, and participated."

"You've got to be kidding," the Washington boys laughed.

"No, no, no, not that unique fellow," Biffy astutely analyzed the character with which they were dealing. "Not consistent with who he is."

"Unredeemable," Stacey was quick to add.

Individuals reported that they thought they spotted the Wily One wearing a Groucho Marx mask, hiding behind its fake nose, black-rimmed glasses, and bushy eyebrows. There were many sighting rumors; however, nothing was confirmed. To be sure, Wigglesworth was elusive and evasive—and extremely good at both!

Chapter 9: More News

Good news: In early November, the two US senators called a press conference and reappeared with state officials to issue a message that gave a lift to the heart of every Ludwigshaven resident—and soon after to the millions following the unfolding saga. SEA's national Superslime Project would clean up the factory grounds and, over time, restore the soil, water, and air to its pristine beauty. Hurrah!

And Biffy, Stacey, and the Wrights were cited for their tenacity and leadership.

"The residents of Ludwigshaven have given voice to the voiceless: the marsh grasses that will once again swish and sway in the pristine tidal flow, the sea creatures that should and will be able to prowl and propel in clean waters," Wolfgang wrote.

"Bravo to all for going to battle for the sustenance of tiny pipers that dash along the beaches and for the feathered gulls that swoop down to dine on uncontaminated sea cuisine," he added. His detailed story of recent developments was a breaking news article on the front page of the *Washington Patriot*, the leading paper in the nation's capital.

"Time to give *thanks*," Biffy said quietly, obviously deeply moved, as cameras clicked and flashes of light popped intermittently.

"What a relief. We are simply *very* grateful and *thankful*," Stacey seconded as tears streamed down her cheeks.

Laura happily revised her early cartoon to reflect the update:

AFTER: Ludwigshaven, A scene of natural beauty

BEFORE: Times are changing

The same scene, dominated by Wigglesworth, a large slithering snake with the head of the
Devil, surrounded by bubbling fluids.

The senators announced that Wigglesworth had been vanquished in a court of law. Fined for not cleaning up his property; required to pay $2,000,000 and more.

Laura's cartoon:

Wigglesworth is shown with the body of a long, long serpent sliding in the mud as officers of the law carried away huge bags of his money.

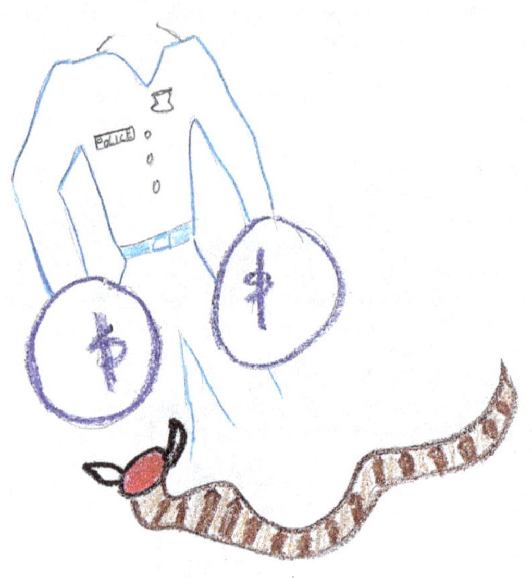

A fine day.

News spread rapidly that the preeminent polluter had lost his suit with the US government.

"Despite all his machinations, delays, and emissaries, he could not and did not escape from the long arm of Uncle Sam," one article began.

The Washington boys took the Wright-the-Wrongs team, now also known also as the Write-the-Wrongs, aside: "We can only imagine how distraught he must be, considering that he was depressed for days after losing a tennis match. But having even a penny of his beloved, precious money taken away? Devastating!"

"An appropriate and fitting result," Biffy added with her usual insight. "Now, he must give up his beloved money."

"In fairness to Wigglesworth, he purchased the factory but did not initially create the chemical catastrophe," Stacey added. "And one could feel sorry for him. He inherited a problem, to say the least, but once in his hands, he could have pitched in, tried to be part of the solution, engaged with us, rather than turning his back, refusing to comply with meetings, and seemingly ignoring the effluent."

"Neither problems nor industrial waste evaporate or disappear by wishful thinking or in absentia," one town official reminded all.

Accordingly, the world press sent out headlines and copy emphasizing the import of the decisions:

Ludwigshaven Is a Role Model for the Country
and the World
Follow the Leaders
How to Save the Planet
Three Cheers for the Team

On and on, all were vying to best describe the successful outcome. Last but not least:

Ludwigshaven Gives Thanks
Thanksgiving in Ludwigshaven

Chapter 10:
An Essential Side Trip

Biffy and Stacey, true to their word, as usual, invited the Wrights to tour the Plimouth Plantation with them. An outdoor museum dedicated to the history of the early settlement we now call Plymouth, the grounds were dotted with exhibitions designed to explain the activities, lifestyles, and interactions of the Native Americans and the English newcomers. Outdoor gardens displayed local agriculture, firepits for cooking, and a small shop sells souvenirs, including Governor Bradford's account.

A Native American, who introduced herself as Halona, greeted them and began her tour by leading them into a large teepee. "My ancestors slept on hammocks and used these brilliantly colored woven rugs, all easily transported as weather conditions changed."

In contrast, an actor representing Governor Bradford led the tourists through small wooden structures, where the immigrant, huddling, transplanted English,; their feather pillows and European furniture were to be protected against the harsh winds and freezing climate.

"The Native Americans were smarter than the conquering white man," Franz observed caustically. "When it rained, they moved under the trees, while the British were constructing shaky wooden structures that the north wind could topple in a blink of an eye. Plus those dirty feather pillows! And the Indians believed in sharing the gifts of nature. I never thought much—or enough—about it before, but now I can easily ask: which was the more adaptable group or civilization? In many respects, I vote for the Native Americans."

Halona smiled, and the actor Governor Bradford explained: "Of course, we interacted, of necessity." He went on to tell of their crossing, hardships, and the death of almost half his fellow travelers. "The Indians taught us to plant corn and celebrated with us at our very first harvest. Much for you to read and learn, and we are here to give you an idea of those difficult and challenging times."

One of the people who had died was Governor Bradford's wife when he was on an expedition from Provincetown to search for a safe harbor. "Why didn't you mention her in your account?" Leonora asked, but the actor Governor Bradford had no answer. Some suggest the subject was too painful for him.

As a parting gift, Halona handed each of the visitors a light beige paper scroll tied in a black ribbon. Unfurling hers, she read the contents aloud to them:

Haudenosaunee Thanksgiving Address: Greetings to the Natural World

The People

Today we have gathered, and we see that the cycles of life continue. We have been given the duty to live in balance and harmony with each other and all living things. So now, we bring our minds together as one as we give greetings and thanks to each other as people.
Now our minds are one.

The Earth Mother

We are all thankful to our Mother, the Earth, for she gives us all that we need for life. She supports our feet as we walk about upon her. It gives us joy that she continues to care for us as she has from the beginning of time. To our mother, we send greetings and thanks.

Now our minds are one.

The Waters

We give thanks to all the waters of the world for quenching our thirst and providing us with strength. Water is life. We know its power in many forms—waterfalls and rain, mists and streams, rivers and oceans. With one mind, we send greetings and thanks to the spirit of Water.

Now our minds are one.

The Fish

We turn our minds to all the fish life in the water. They were instructed to cleanse and purify the water. They also give themselves to us as food. We are grateful that we can still find pure water. So, we turn now to the Fish and send our greetings and thanks.

Now our minds are one.

The Plants

Now we turn toward the vast fields of Plant life. As far as the eye can see, the Plants grow, working many wonders. They sustain many life forms. With our minds gathered together, we give thanks and look forward to seeing Plant life for many generations to come.

Now our minds are one.

The Food Plants

With one mind, we turn to honor and thank all the Food Plants we harvest from the garden.

Since the beginning of time, grains, vegetables, beans, and berries have helped people survive. Many other living things draw strength from them too. We gather all the Plant Foods together as one and send them a greeting of thanks.

Now our minds are one.

The Medicine Herbs

Now we turn to all the Medicine herbs of the world. From the beginning, they were instructed to take away sickness. They are always waiting and ready to heal us. We are happy there are still among us those special few who remember how to use these plants for healing. With one mind, we send greetings and thanks to the Medicines and to the keepers of the Medicines.

Now our minds are one.

The Animals

We gather our minds together to send greetings and thanks to all the Animal life in the world. They have many things to teach us as people. We are honored by them when they give up their lives so we may use their bodies as food for our people. We see them near our homes and in the deep forests. We are glad they are still here, and we hope that it will always be so.

Now our minds are one.

The Trees

We now turn our thoughts to the Trees. The Earth has many families of Trees who have their own instructions and uses. Some provide us with shelter and shade, others with fruit, beauty, and other useful things. Many people of the world use a Tree as a symbol of peace and strength. With one mind, we greet and thank the Tree life.

Now our minds are one.

The Birds

We put our minds together as one and thank all the Birds who move and fly about over our heads. The Creator gave them beautiful songs. Each day, they remind us to enjoy and appreciate life. The Eagle was chosen to be their leader. To all the Birds—from the smallest to the largest—we send our joyful greetings and thanks.

Now our minds are one.

The Four Winds

We are all thankful to the powers we know as the Four Winds. We hear their voices in the moving air as they refresh us and purify the air we breathe. They help us bring the change of seasons. From the four directions, they come, bringing us messages and giving us strength. With one mind, we send our greetings and thanks to the Four Winds.

Now our minds are one.

The Thunderers

Now we turn to the west, where our grandfathers, the Thunder Beings, live. With lightning and thundering voices, they bring with them the water that renews life. We are thankful that they keep those evil things made by Okwiseres underground. We bring our minds together as one to send greetings and thanks to our Grandfathers, the Thunderers.

Now our minds are one.

The Sun

We now send greetings and thanks to our eldest Brother, the Sun. Each day without fail, he travels the sky from east to west, bringing the light of a new day. He is the source of all the fires of life. With one mind, we send greetings and thanks to our Brother, the Sun.

Now our minds are one.

Grandmother Moon

We put our minds together to give thanks to our oldest Grandmother, the Moon, who lights the nighttime sky. She is the leader of woman all over the world, and she governs the movement of the ocean tides. By her changing face, we measure time, and it is the Moon who watches over the arrival of children here on Earth. With one mind, we send greetings and thanks to our Grandmother, the Moon.

Now our minds are one.

The Stars

We give thanks to the Stars who are spread across the sky like jewelry. We see them in the night, helping the Moon to light the darkness and bringing dew to the gardens and growing things. When we travel at night, they guide us home. With our minds gathered together as one, we send greetings and thanks to the Stars.

Now our minds are one.

The Enlightened Teachers

We gather our minds to greet and thank the enlightened Teachers who have come to help throughout the ages. When we forget how to live in harmony, they remind us of the way we were instructed to live as people. With one mind, we send greetings and thanks to these caring teachers.

Now our minds are one.

The Creator

Now we turn our thoughts to the Creator, or Great Spirit, and send greetings and thanks for all the gifts of Creation. Everything we need to live a good life is here on this Mother Earth. For all the love that is still around us, we gather our minds together as one and send our choicest words of greetings and thanks to the Creator.

Now our minds are one.

Closing Words

We have now arrived at the place where we end our words. Of all the things we have named, it was not our intention to leave anything out. If something was forgotten, we leave it to each individual to send such greetings and thanks in their own way.

Now our minds are one.

"A beautiful message, very moving," Biffy responded. "Lots to think about. My ancestors came on the Mayflower, and I can only imagine what really transpired. In our time, this message is very important. We should all take to heart the content, especially given how human beings can forget what is precious and right."

"And here is a shorter one," Halona handed them each a second scroll tied in a red ribbon and read aloud from hers:

An Iroquois Prayer

We return thanks to our mother, the earth, which sustains us.

We return thanks to the rivers and streams, which supply us with water.

We return thanks to all herbs, which furnish medicines for the cure of our diseases.

We return thanks to the corn and to her sisters, the beans and squash, which give us life.

We return thanks to the bushes and trees, which provide us with fruit.

We return thanks to the wind, which moving the air, has banished diseases.

We return thanks to the moon and the stars, which have given us their light when the sun was gone.

We return thanks to our grandfather He-no, who has protected his children the fish and the reptiles and has given us his rain.

We return thanks to the sun, that he has looked upon the earth with a beneficent eye.

Lastly, we return thanks to the Great Spirit, in whom is embodied all goodness, and directs all things for the good of his children.

"What a contrast to the way of life of the English," Franz commented.

"Yes, and much to discuss. When we get swept up in our busy lives," Wolfgang responded as they said goodbye, "first, let's all stop and be thankful for so many things we take for granted in nature and life. That was a great tour and an eye-opener. Thank you!"

"And thanks to you, Biffy and Stacey, for taking us here, back into American history," Laura added.

Biffy and Stacey smiled knowingly.

Chapter 11: Thanksgiving

How to celebrate the good news from the SEA and the start of the long-awaited cleanup? Why, in the way they knew best in Ludwigshaven: a Thanksgiving like the old days! What better and more appropriate way to observe and recognize being plucked from disaster by human ingenuity and fellowship?

Town officials announced a commemoration in which Biffy, Stacey, and the Wrights would be honored and every citizen would participate. A feast for all would be enjoyed in the town square, reminiscent of and harkening back to Mr. Ludwig's spread. The band would shatter the air and play after the football game to entertain the families.

Plus more good news: a surprise! No expense would be spared, thanks to the extraordinary donation of the Cheerables, a wealthy family living on the other side of the country and following developments in the news. So inspired, they would be traveling 3,000 miles to join in the marking of the renewal and reinvigoration at Ludwigshaven's Thanksgiving Day Celebration.

Once again, for the first time in decades, on the last Thursday of November, Ludwigshavians gathered together. With many compliments and congratulatory remarks, Jay and Marian Cheerable, relatives of the famous Cheerable Brothers, joined in the ceremonies, taking turns addressing the assembled crowd and photo-popping press.

"Your story has inspired and uplifted us and many others. Thank you!" Jay Cheerable spoke, his bass voice thundering from a microphone and speakers on the makeshift stage erected for the event as he enunciated every word slowly and carefully.

"You have impressed us by your working together and dedication to protect human and animal life, sea creatures, and natural beauty," he continued. "You are a model for others who can learn from you and follow in your footsteps, to fight for what is right and important. We fled from Communist China and have had the good fortune to become Americans, to thrive in our economy, and we appreciate your unity and struggle. In our marvelous melting pot of immigrants, we must all work together for the common good."

"We are funding this celebration and giving you a grant in perpetuity for generations to come. Here is a copy of the binding legal document to ensure such an annual festivity," Marian Cheerable took over, waving sheets of paper in the cool, crisp fall air. "You are an example for the nation and the world. Let this story be told across the land, and may others learn from your efforts, methods, triumphs, and successes and be motivated to protect our country and planet."

After not too many official speeches of thanks from Ludwigshavians, Jay spoke again: "We have a request: Inclusion. A thought, on this occasion, heard 'round the world. A simple word and thought, but not so easily implemented in human society and history. To us, that means making sure Thanksgiving is a celebration for *all*—and I mean *all*, regardless of race, religion, creed, background, and political views.

"The history of Thanksgiving is complicated. The world of Charles Ludwig was different in many ways from our time. He loved Thanksgiving and paid tribute to those who survived after their dangerous, arduous, and daring trip on the Mayflower, but I don't have to tell you that times change.

"Now, many speak about the early settlers' treatment of the Native Americans and insensitivity to their plight for centuries. National Mourning Day vigils are held to protest Thanksgiving celebrations. Atheists ask provocatively: 'If there is no God, to whom are you giving thanks?'

"Every generation experiences new challenges and overcomes new adversities. And we look back on the past, often wondering how those before us managed or thought and did what they did—often things we would call reprehensible now.

"This Thanksgiving Day is a perfect time for inclusion, for a new start, for overcoming differences, and for coming together. Each of us has something to be thankful for: life, liberty, the pursuit of happiness to begin with . . . and much more if we stop to think about our lives.

"Marian and I are suggesting that we *all* come together, update, and include *all* our citizens with respect, dignity, dialogue, and understanding. Ludwigshaven is a good place from which to create *a new and renewed understanding of a holiday treasured by millions but reshaped in light of our diverse population.* A focal point for discussion and resolution of differences. A wonderful day for all." Jay stopped speaking and handed the microphone to Marian.

"When we look back in history, we learn that harvest festivals date back to antiquity, including reference to the Tabernacle in the Bible," she noted. "The English brought such a tradition to our shores, right near here—literally! On their first Thanksgiving, they were joined by Native Americans.

"Over the years, celebrations and traditions have changed. George Washington, at the request of Congress, issued a proclamation for a 'Day of Publick Thanksgivin' in 1789. Dates varied for decades, and not until Abraham Lincoln was a specific day earmarked for the annual celebration. Historians tell us that a woman, writer, and editor, Sarah Josepha Hale, encouraged President

Lincoln to declare a national holiday to unite the country during the Civil War, urging him to create a permanent American custom and institution. A woman's influence!" Marian beamed.

"But the saga didn't end there. Even under President Franklin Roosevelt, for a time, there were two different Thursdays celebrated by different states. Only in 1941 did Congress establish a federal Thanksgiving holiday on the fourth Thursday of November.

"Human beings adapt and update," Marian continued. "Let Ludwigshaven be an example because of its past history and its current activities and international reputation. Inclusion. From this podium in Ludwigshaven, we are urging *all* people across this land to *join together* on this day, to treat Thanksgiving Day literally—as a day of *giving thanks*. A day and time to take note of and celebrate the good, the many blessings and gifts we have and share now."

Applause and cheers from the audience lasted for several minutes.

"We have one more proposal, a small suggestion for a new tradition. Each year, as part of your ceremony, please share and read aloud inspiring words that underscore hopeful, inclusive, peaceful messages. To begin, Leonora and Franz have chosen a beautiful, suitable Thanksgiving message."

The twins ascended to the podium, along with their new friend, Halona. Their voices soared over the crowd as they introduced her.

"My name Halona means Happy Fortune," she said, taking the microphone. "And it is my happy fortune to be here to celebrate with you today."

Calmly, with great dignity, she unrolled her scroll and recited the "Haudenosaunee Thanksgiving Address: Greetings to the Natural World." Her words were broadcast across the earth.

When she concluded, the audience sat quietly at first, pensive, and soon joined in thunderous applause and cheering. Small paper booklets were being passed to every individual as Leonora read The Iroquois Prayer.

"The booklet you are receiving is a gift from us. It has both texts and one more important message, a favorite of ours," Marian explained. "My family and I have chosen the words from the final speech of the great American classic film *The Great Dictator* by Charlie Chaplin. We would like to include favorite excerpts that are very moving and touching—reflect our feelings about this joyous occasion."

In clear resounding tones, she read, with press sending her voice too around the world:

I should like to help everyone—if possible.

We all want to help one another. Human beings are like that.

We want to live by each other's happiness— not by each other's misery.

We don't want to hate and despise one another. In this world, there is room for everyone. And the good earth is rich and can provide for everyone.

The way of life can be free and beautiful, but we have lost the way.

Greed has poisoned men's souls . . .

Our knowledge has made us cynical. Our cleverness, hard and unkind.

We think too much and feel too little.

More than machinery, we need humanity.

More than cleverness, we need kindness and gentleness.

Without these qualities, life will be violent, and all will be lost . . .

The aeroplane and the radio have brought us closer together.

The very nature of these inventions cries out for the goodness in men—cries out for universal brotherhood—for the unity of us all.

. . . liberty will never perish . . .

You have the love of humanity in your hearts! You don't hate!

Only the unloved hate—the unloved and the unnatural!

You, the people, have the power—the power to create machines

The power to create happiness! You, the people, have the power to make this life free and beautiful, to make this life a wonderful adventure.

Let us all unite. Let us fight for a new world—a decent world that will give men a chance to work, that will give youth a future, and old age a security.

Let us fight to free the world—to do away with . . . barriers, to do away with greed, with hate and intolerance.

Let us fight for a world of reason, a world where science and progress will lead to all men's happiness.

Biffy rose and took the microphone.

"What meaningful thoughts. What important messages for this time and for all time. We cannot repeat often enough that we have so much to be grateful for. We thank the Cheerables, we thank the Wrights, we thank you fellow Ludwigshavians, and you, senators, who are with us today."

"A toast to you, Biffy Revere!" The senators raised their cider glasses in unison. "And to you, Stacey Lincoln, for leading your fellow citizens. The eyes of the world are watching, and ears and minds are glued to your words."

"Thank you, thank you. I am deeply honored," Biffy responded with quiet strength and modesty. "On behalf of all our fellow Ludwigshaven citizens, Stacey and I thank you for your interest and efforts. There are many good people all over the country and the world, struggling as best they can with problems and challenges. Trying to be heard, to change difficult situations and problems. So-called 'little people,' which is code for average citizens who have little power and savvy to battle powerful polluters. But our town has been particularly lucky because amazing, generous, wonderful people have stepped in and helped us. We are fortunate that the press has singled us out for extensive coverage, getting our story out.

"A special thanks to our new neighbors, Wolfgang and Laura Wright and their twins, who have helped shine a spotlight on our local issue. We are being called a beacon, reassuring little towns, big cities, and countries alike that we can work together to overcome enormous challenges," Stacey added. "And we are a tiny reflection of the melting pot of America with our various backgrounds: Native American, Mayflower descendant, Eastern European immigrant, descendants of slaves, European, and Asian, plus . . ."

"POP," Marian Cheerable interjected, holding up large orange metal campaign-style buttons with the black letters *POP* encircled by the word *Ludwigshaven.* "POP stands for power of the pen/press. Another thing to celebrate and give thanks for is our free press, which led us to you. We have plenty to go around, one for each of you, using the town colors, of course. Just hitch them on like this." She demonstrated, attaching one to her jacket. "Something else to remember to give thanks for."

After more toasts and speeches, the band played, and the feast began. Games, dancing, and socializing continued until that beautiful fall day ended with a magnificent sunset illuminating the sky with orange hues that gradually disappeared into inky-black darkness. A new tradition had begun.

Chapter 12: Aftermath

True to Wolfgang's early expectations, the SEA and the government moved slowly to rectify the damage resulting from decades of pollution. Step by step.

One official explained that "he would need a hazy crystal ball to try and predict just when residents would be able to sit along the harbor with a fishing rod in hand. There is about a ten-year lag between cleanup and safe-to-eat seafood."

In an article about upcoming plans, Wolfgang communicated what he had learned from official postings about the Superslime Project:

"The law requires companies and individuals responsible for the contaminated site to perform and pay for the investigation and cleanup. If those responsible are unwilling to cooperate, the SEA can issue an order requiring them to do the cleanup, or the SEA can do the work often in cooperation with the State with funds from

Congress. Once the cleanup is complete, the SEA can seek to recover costs. There are settlements."

Step by step: First, there is an official process for such a toxic site, beginning with a regional contact and a hazardous ranking score. To follow are discovery, site inspection, preliminary assessment, listing on the National Priority List, and removal.

Here is a chronology of what actually transpired subsequently, according to official reports:

> 2000: Superslime National Priority Listing by SEA with a cleanup plan finalized.

> 2000: Super Environment Agency (SEA) cleaned up asbestos.

> 2002: Ludwigshaven records showed the Ludwig Factory had not paid taxes since 1990—$18,000 owed, plus interest.

> 2003: The US government agency SEA filed suit against Ludwig Factory and its President Wigglesworth for $25,000,000 needed for cleanup.

> 2005: SEA began cleanup, demolition of collapsing structures, removal of contaminated soil, groundwater monitoring, and site restoration.

2006: Wigglesworth was fined. The agreement included the following: The town was paid back taxes! The property could be sold with 97% of proceeds going to the government, or ownership could be retained, paying US 97% of the fair market value. The town of Ludwigshaven agreed to pay unpaid real estate taxes. It would collect over $80,000 to be used for cleanup.

Six sites were listed: four owned by Ludwig Factory, one by Wigglesworth, and one by Big Deals Industries.

2007: Ludwigshaven Superslime Project was completed, and monitoring began. Five-year reviews were planned.

2021: SEA began working across the country with owners of Superslime Projects to implement controls, ensuring future reuse consistent with cleanup and protection of human health and environment.

End to a problem that held the town on the brink of environmental disaster for years.

The change was slow and took years. Although the cleanup ended officially in September 2007, the SEA continued to monitor the location at five-year intervals to ensure the environmental conditions did not worsen.

After careful and seemingly endless work, the Ludwig Factory property was restored to its natural state and rededicated as a public nature preserve, a monument to its pristine past when the Native Americans met the first settlers. A protected, safe haven in which all creatures—human, animal, insect, and aviary—can flourish and thrive.

The headlines across the nation were variations on a theme:

> Historic New England Town, Once Plagued by Factory's Toxic Pollution, Enjoys Revitalized Coastal Marshes

> Agencies Work Together to Preserve and Create Fresh and Saltwater Wetlands at Former Manufacturing Facility

A tale with a happy ending echoing across the borders of a great nation and boomeranging from continent to continent. Truly the inspiration and role model, as intended and lauded.

Chapter 13: Today

Thanksgiving Day has continued to be a festive annual celebration in Ludwigshaven, with many other towns and locales influenced and imitating.

"Imitation is the greatest form of flattery," Biffy jokes, happy to share her joy with others.

The words "Give Thanks" are chosen by Biffy and Stacey and inscribed in large letters above their names and images on the Town Mothers Monument erected in front of the library. Laura does the preliminary drawings for the sculptor.

The plaque below reads: "In honor of Biffy Revere and Stacey Lincoln and the team, courageous citizens and leaders, fighters for justice and the environment."

Around the base are five additional small sculptures: the four Wrights with their names. And if you look closely, there is a tiny cat. The unsuspecting might think the little creature was simply a decorative addition, but those in the know recognize a tribute to Peanut Butter, whose paws decidedly brought them together and helped launch a local revolution.

On Thanksgiving, their story is told in homes and religious institutions across the nation in remembrance of the land and gifts we have inherited from our forefathers.

As time passed, Wigglesworth has become but a faint memory, isolated, clawing perhaps. Or maybe he is resting on his laurels and loot, having crawled back into the elegant woodwork of his various homes, a private citizen, forgotten. His legacy, the opposite of what he had intended.

"Who would want to know such a person anyway?" Biffy reminisces.

"The people gave thanks to be rid of him—yet a new reason to give thanks!" Stacey jokes.

"John Milton in *Paradise Lost* was perplexed about how even a snake, the Devil, could evade all-powerful God and slip away. In the eternal battle between good and evil, there are those who are unredeemed, unredeemable, and carry on in their evil ways," Biffy responds in her philosophical way. "Not much we can do about that."

Postcards are sold in the Village Store to tourists who visit, with pictures of the Town Mothers Monument, various Ludwig buildings, Laura's cartoons, and the marshes. There are also playing cards with similar images and Thanksgiving messages booklets.

An entrepreneurial resident has created Biffy, Stacey, and Wright family dolls and toys, sold across the nation for Thanksgiving gifts. High school students have invented a game called Ecopoly, with Ludwigshaven as the focal point and the factory and other local sites as content. If you throw the dice and have to move your cat to the factory, you are in real trouble; you lose the game. The board game is for sale, too, with proceeds supporting the science programs in the schools.

Leonora is a respected and admired professor and teacher, the author of numerous books on the environment. She has created school projects about the environment, which are used across the country. Subjects include improving air quality, the use of native plants, erosion, wildlife habitats, wetlands, woodlands, sustainable energy, transportation choices, food waste and recycling, and of course, pollution.

Her most recent book, *A History of the Ludwigshaven Debacle*, was reviewed and praised widely: "Agencies work together to preserve and create fresh and saltwater wetlands at a world-renowned manufacturing facility." A new addition to the gifts one can purchase in the Village Store and from booksellers everywhere.

Franz is an oceanographer, and his list of projects includes saving whales, consulting on oil spills, supervising photography of the deep, studying water currents and aquaculture, and teaching students each summer at Woods Hole. At a recent speech at the UN, he projected his mother's latest cartoon showing him disentangling a mallard's leg from a pile of floating debris.

Biffy, at close to 100, is often sitting on her porch in a rocking chair, surrounded by admirers who now do the rose clipping and other errands for her. She is loved, listened to, and cared for by those to whom she gave so much.

Stacey and her family continue to participate in town life and help newcomers adjust. The Wrights remain their close friends; the generations spend time socializing and travel together with their families.

According to the town census, the population of Ludwigshaven is composed of citizens who are white, African American, Asian, American Indian and Alaska Native, Native Hawaiian, and others.

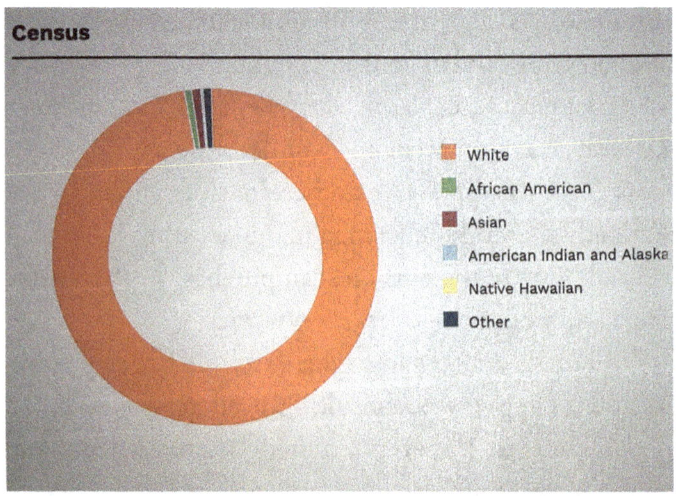

Not exactly as diverse as big cities in America, but it is gradually changing, all the while spreading the messages of unity, giving, sharing, caring, and influencing millions. A small but powerful example of how a tiny dot of a town and a handful of dedicated, effective human beings can initiate new ways of interacting and change the world.

Postscript: Recently, while browsing and researching, Leonora has located the following questions on the Ludwig Factory Superslime Site with answers from the SEA.

Q: What is a brownfield?

A brownfield is any land in the United States that is abandoned, idled, or underused because redevelopment and/or expansion is complicated by environmental contamination that is either real or perceived. Brownfields differ from Superslime sites in the degree of contamination. Superslime sites pose a real threat to human health and/or the environment. Brownfields, on the other hand, do not pose a serious health or environmental threat. Instead, they represent an economic or social threat since they prevent development. Therefore, they stifle local economies. The federal government continues to have enforcement authority in all cases, and the SEA has oversight responsibility for the states' activities, monitoring state and tribal implementation of SEA-approved programs.

SEA works cooperatively with the states and tribes to better achieve effective enforcement and environmental compliance and continues to support approved state programs through grant funding and sharing the work.

Q: What's the difference between vent gas and waste gas?

Waste gas is the gas from a processing unit destined for disposal. Vent gas is the mixture of all gases and vapors that are present at the exit but just inside the flare tip.

The questions appear to have come from Wigglesworth, and Leonora has been wondering if he and Wilhelmina are considering doing something to the property owned or wished to own. Could it be that he can benefit from the cleanup now in a new way?

Is the King of Slime in his counting/country house counting out his money?

Is Wilhelmina in the parlor, eating bread and honey?

Biffy, Stacey, and the Wrights long ago prepared a surprise, a tell-tale pie, and the birds began to sing.

Wasn't that a dainty dish to set before the king?

Thanksgiving Address: Greetings to the Natural World

- English version: John Stokes and Kanawahienton (David Benedict, Turtle Clan/Mohawk)
- Mohawk version: Rokwaho (Dan Thompson, Wolf Clan/Mohawk)
- Original inspiration: Tekaronianekon (Jake Swamp, Wolf Clan/Mohawk)

(Note: The translation of the Mohawk version of the Haudenosaunee Thanksgiving Address was published in 1993 and provided, courtesy of the Six Nations Indian Museum and the Tracking Project. All rights reserved.)

About the Author

Dr. Joan Thomson Kretschmer, Artistic Director and founder of the Lyric Chamber Music Society of New York, attended Smith College and graduated from Barnard College, where she majored in political science. In conjunction with her interests in politics and human nature, she focused on music and received her M.A. and Ph.D. in musicology from Columbia University, where she was a Clarence Barker Fellow.

Joan is the author of *YONA: Discoveries, Doorways, and Musical Superpower* in which Yona discovers her supernatural musical abilities that can transform human behavior. She has written *Michelangela and Debuts*, a book of short stories, and other works. *Yona Goes To The Magic Flute* is an adventure to the Metropolitan Opera to learn about Mozart and test her powers. All are available on Amazon and elsewhere. Please visit Joan's website at: JoanKretschmer.com.

She has been a music critic for *The New York Post* and has written articles about music for *The New York Times,*

Opera News, Stagebill, Keynote, The Greenwich Time, and other publications. Her program notes have appeared at concerts at Mostly Mozart, at the Metropolitan Museum of Art, and elsewhere.

At The New School for Social Research, Dr. Kretschmer created and hosted *Musicians on Music,* a series of interviews with artists Daniel Barenboim, Victor Borge, the Guarneri String Quartet, Marilyn Horne, Zubin Mehta, Birgit Nilsson, Jean-Pierre Rampal, Peter Schickele, André Watts, Robert Merrill, and others. She has taught at The Juilliard School and lectured at the SUNY at Purchase and for the Metropolitan Opera Guild. At Yale University, she directed an *Oral History of Electronics in Music,* a collection of interviews with significant innovators in twentieth-century musical life. In addition to writing scripts for radio and national broadcasts of The Richard Tucker Gala, she hosted *Upbeat,* her own classical music radio show.

A grateful student of pianist Jascha Zayde, she has performed with wind and string players from the New York Philharmonic, including Joseph Robinson, Principal Oboe, and Sheryl Staples, Principal Associate Concert Master.

Joan was the music consultant on the award-winning film "Le Refuge" by writer/director Elliot Thomson and for *Vincent Van Gogh: A Portrait in Two Parts.* As an active educator, she gives piano lessons and music classes to all age groups in her studio near Lincoln Center.